W9-AZG-425

Dewey Doo-it™
Feeds a Friend

By Brahm Wenger & Alan Green   Illustrated by Jean Gillmore

Dedicated to Larry and Frances Jones who turned one of life's interruptions into an opportunity to feed hungry children throughout the world.

Library of Congress Control Number: 2003097167

Dewey Doo-it is a registered trademark of The Helpful Doo-its Project LLC.
Published by RandallFraser Publishing
2082 Business Center Drive, Suite 163
Irvine, CA 92612
Printed in Korea

Here’s Dewey Doo-it!

One summer day Dewey invited his friend Marty to play ring-toss in the park with his older brother Howie Doo-it and their friend Kenya Doo-it.

Soon they were joined by the twins Woody Doo-it and Willie Doo-it and Dewey's little sister Anita Doo-it.

Marty was very fast. He darted around catching all the rings. Up, up, up they went. Red. Blue. Orange. Green. The Doo-its played ring-toss with Marty every day that summer.

But one day Marty didn't come to play.
"Where is he?" asked Dewey. "He's never been late for ring-toss before."
"I wonder what's keeping him," said Howie.
"I'm sure he'll show up soon," said Kenya.

But he never did.

Dewey was worried. He hiked across the valley and climbed up the big hill to the place where Marty lived.

There he found his friend leaning against an old hollow log.

"Where have you been?" Dewey asked. "Don't you like playing ring-toss with us anymore?"

Marty looked very sad. "Sorry Dewey," Marty sighed. "I'm too tired to come down the hill to play."

"Tired?" Dewey said. "Maybe you should take a nap."

"No!" Marty cried, "I don't need a nap. I need food! I haven't had anything to eat for days. I'm tired because I'm hungry!"

Dewey was shocked. He looked up at Marty's fruit tree. "What happened to all your food?" he asked.

“A few days ago, a cold wind came swooping out of the night sky and blew away all my fruit!” Marty explained. “Everything’s gone now.”

Marty was in trouble. But Dewey had an idea.

"I know where I can find lots of food for you," Dewey yelled, as he ran down the big hill. "Don't worry. I'll be back soon."

Dewey ran all the way back across the valley to the park where he knew there was a fruit tree with lots of juicy apples and oranges and mangos and mellons. But no matter how hard he tried, no matter how high he jumped, *Dewey Doo-it couldn't do it*.

Soon Dewey's older brother Howie came by to see if he could help.
"That fruit is much too high up in the tree for us to reach," Howie said.
Just then Dewey noticed a group of ants nearby doing something very strange.

"Look at that!" Dewey said. "Those tiny ants have given me a wonderful idea. We need teamwork! We need our friends!"

Dewey helped Kenya, Woody, Willie and Anita climb up on each other's shoulders – just like the ants.

The tree was very tall and the Doo-its were very small, but that didn't bother them at all. Soon they made a food chain to pass the juicy apples and oranges and mangos and mellons to Howie so he could put them in the wagon.

Dewey then hurried off to his house. "We need to get much more food for Marty!" he called out. "Go over and pick some vegetables from the garden. I'll meet you there."

Two by two, the Doo-its loaded the zucchinis and cucumbers into the wagon.

"Marty's going to love this giant carrot," said Kenya.

Just as they finished, Dewey arrived with a big white box. "Okay Doo-its. Let's roll!"

The helpful Doo-its were ready to start their long journey.

Slowly they pushed and pulled the heavy wagon through the Jingle Jangle Jungle all the way up the big hill to Marty's.

It was such hard work, even the tiny ants pitched in to help.

The hill was so steep that the mangos, melons and tomatoes kept falling off the back of the wagon.

"I'm too tired to push anymore," Woody said.

"Let's stop," said Kenya. "I need to rest."

"NO!" called Dewey. "We can't stop now, Marty's very weak. He's waiting for us to save him!" He turned to Kenya and assured her, *"You can do it, Kenya Doo-it!"*

Finally, the helpful Doo-its made it to the top of the big hill.

"Shhhh!" Dewey whispered. "Look, Marty's sleeping. Let's unload the food and surprise him."

There were lots of fruits and vegetables left over, so Kenya and the twins stored them in Marty's old hollow log. "That should last him till his tree grows more fruit," they said.

“Now I think it’s time for a certain turtle to wake up,” Dewey said. “Okay everybody, one...two...three....”

"SURPRISE!"

"Oh, wow!" Marty said. "Look what you brought me!"
Hurray! *Dewey Doo-it finally did it!*
Marty happily munched on all the mangos, melons and tomatoes.

“We have one more surprise for you,” Dewey said. “And I bet you’ll never guess what it is.”

What could be in the big white box?

"It's a ring-toss cake!" everyone cheered. Dewey Doo-it and the other helpful Doo-its couldn't wait to play ring-toss again. But for now, they were all just happy to gather round and have a big slice of ring-toss cake... and party with Marty.

Hi Everyone!

Wasn't that a wonderful story? I loved helping my friend Marty when he had no food! This story was inspired by another person who helps people who have no food. His name is Larry Jones.

In 1979, on a trip to Haiti, Larry Jones met a little Haitian boy named Jerry. Jerry asked Larry Jones if he had a nickel. The boy had not eaten all day, and a nickel, he explained, would buy a roll … three more cents would butter both sides!

Meeting that little boy, who asked for so little and needed so much, was a turning point for Larry Jones. He knew then that he needed to help the thousands of children who were hungry all around the world. Together with his wife, Frances, Larry created Feed The Children. Larry found some friends to help him, and then he found more friends until he had enough helpers to gather the extra food here in America and take it to hungry children in this country, in Haiti, and in other places around the world.

Today, Larry's group of friends has grown very large and has made it possible for Feed The Children to reach millions of hungry children in more than 100 countries. With his friends and Feed The Children's big trucks, Larry can quickly send food, medicine, clothing, educational books and other supplies to people who need help.

It all started with one hungry little boy, and one man who wanted to help. This example of how one person can change the world inspired *Dewey Doo-it Feeds a Friend.*

Thanks, Dewey

If you would like to help Larry Jones feed the children, contact:
Feed The Children P.O. Box 36 Oklahoma City, OK 73101
800-627-4556 www.feedthechildren.org.